GRAPHIC MYTHICAL CREATURES

OGRES

BY GARY JEFFREY
ILLUSTRATED BY JAMES FIELD

Gareth Stevens
Publishing

Please visit our website, www.garethstevens.com.
For a free color catalog of all our high-quality books,
call toll free 1-800-542-2595 or fax 1-877-542-2596.

Library of Congress Cataloging-in-Publication Data

Jeffrey, Gary.
Ogres / Gary Jeffrey.
p. cm. — (Graphic mythical creatures)
Includes index.
ISBN 978-1-4339-6039-0 (pbk.)
ISBN 978-1-4339-6040-6 (6-pack)
ISBN 978-1-4339-6037-6 (library binding)
1. Ghouls and ogres. I. Title.
GR560.J435 2011
398.21—dc22

2010054377

First Edition

Published in 2012 by
Gareth Stevens Publishing
111 East 14th Street, Suite 349
New York, NY 10003

Designed by David West Books
Editor: Ronne Randall

Printed in China

compliance information: Batch #DS11GS: For further information contact Gareth Stevens, New York, New York at 1-800-542-2595.

CONTENTS

MEAN AND GREEN

Many children know about ogres from the movie character Shrek. At worst, Shrek is only smelly and bad tempered. A much scarier, nastier creature lurks in the pages of fairy tales and history books.

The modern-day notion of an ogre is an ugly, swamp-dwelling giant with green skin and an attitude problem.

WHAT MAKES AN OGRE?

Ogres are human-like and represent the darker side of human nature. Often giant sized, they are always hideously ugly and are usually very strong. Greedy treasure hoarders, ogres like to eat people and have a keen sense of smell for humans.

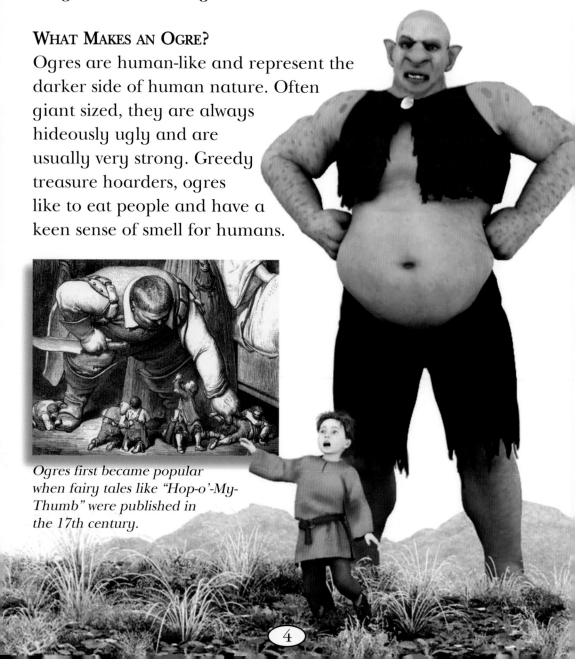

Ogres first became popular when fairy tales like "Hop-o'-My-Thumb" were published in the 17th century.

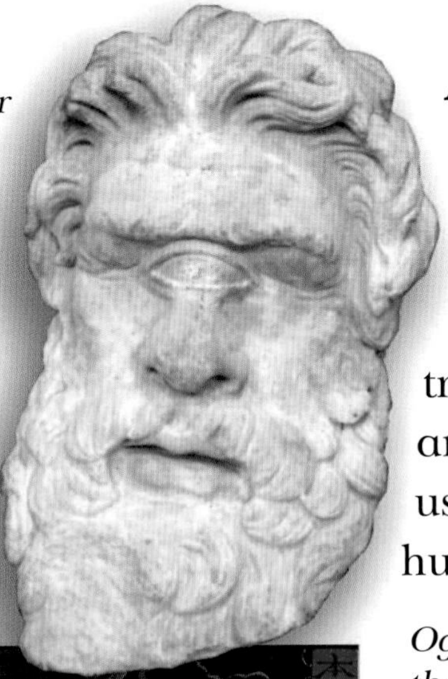

The ancient Greek monster Cyclops was a forerunner of the ogre of fairy tales.

A Taste for Flesh

Many mythological giants, like the one-eyed Cyclops, preyed on humans. The difference is that ogres *always* try to eat people. Luckily, they are not terribly smart and can usually be outwitted by superior human cunning.

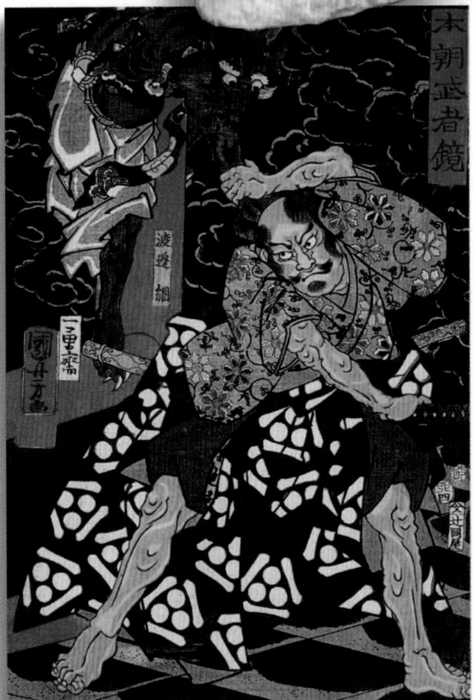
本朝武者鏡

A Japanese print shows the Ogre of Rashomon fighting a knight.

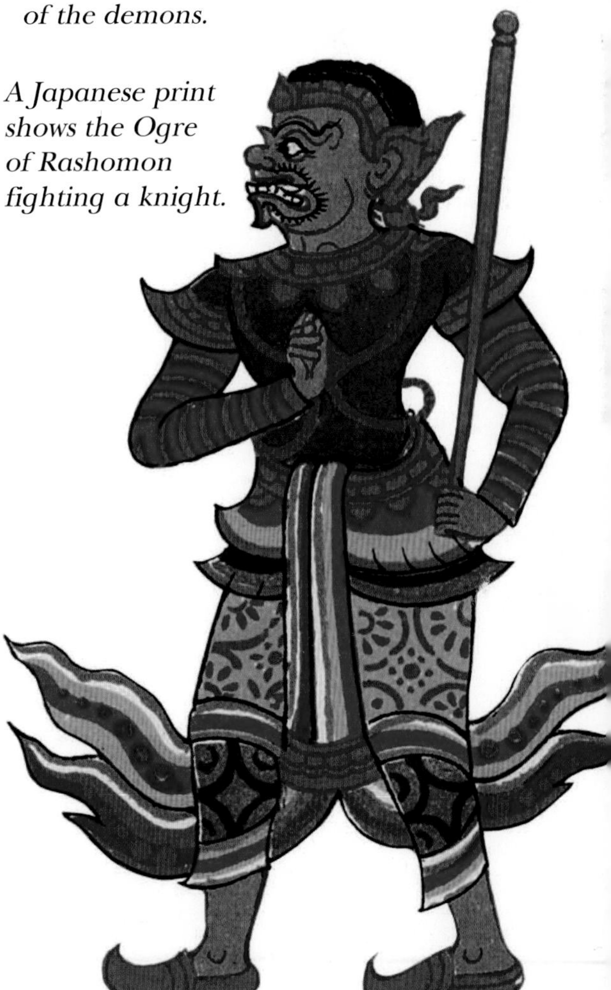

Ogres are found in mythologies around the world. This is an ogre from Burma (or Myanmar) called Kumbhanda—chief of the demons.

Japanese Ogres

Japanese ogres are called oni. Oni were fearsome demons. Hairy and horned, oni often carried spiked clubs into battle against their enemies—the Japanese knights called samurai.

Tom Hickathrift and the Ogre of Tilney Marsh

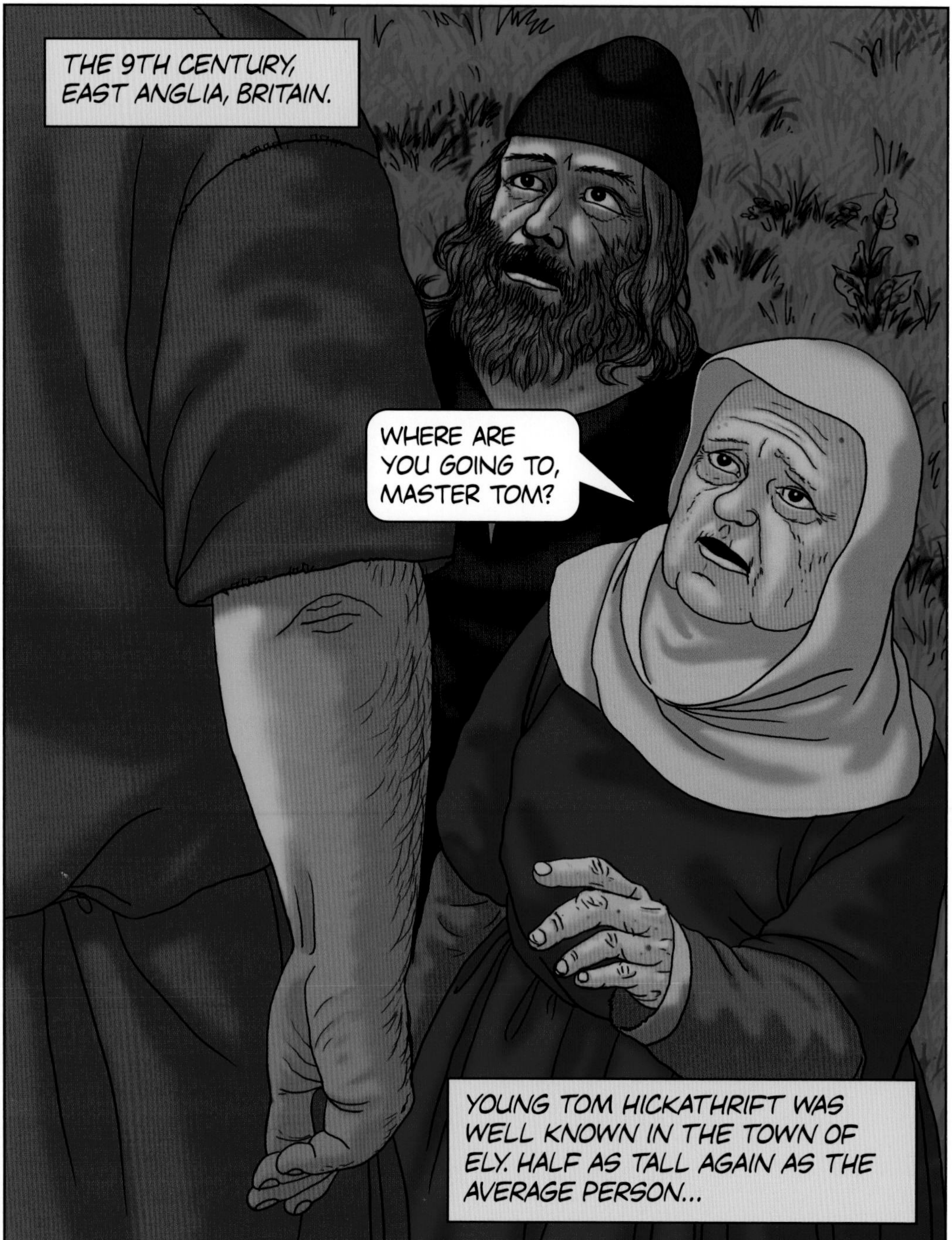
THE 9TH CENTURY, EAST ANGLIA, BRITAIN.
WHERE ARE YOU GOING TO, MASTER TOM?
YOUNG TOM HICKATHRIFT WAS WELL KNOWN IN THE TOWN OF ELY. HALF AS TALL AGAIN AS THE AVERAGE PERSON...

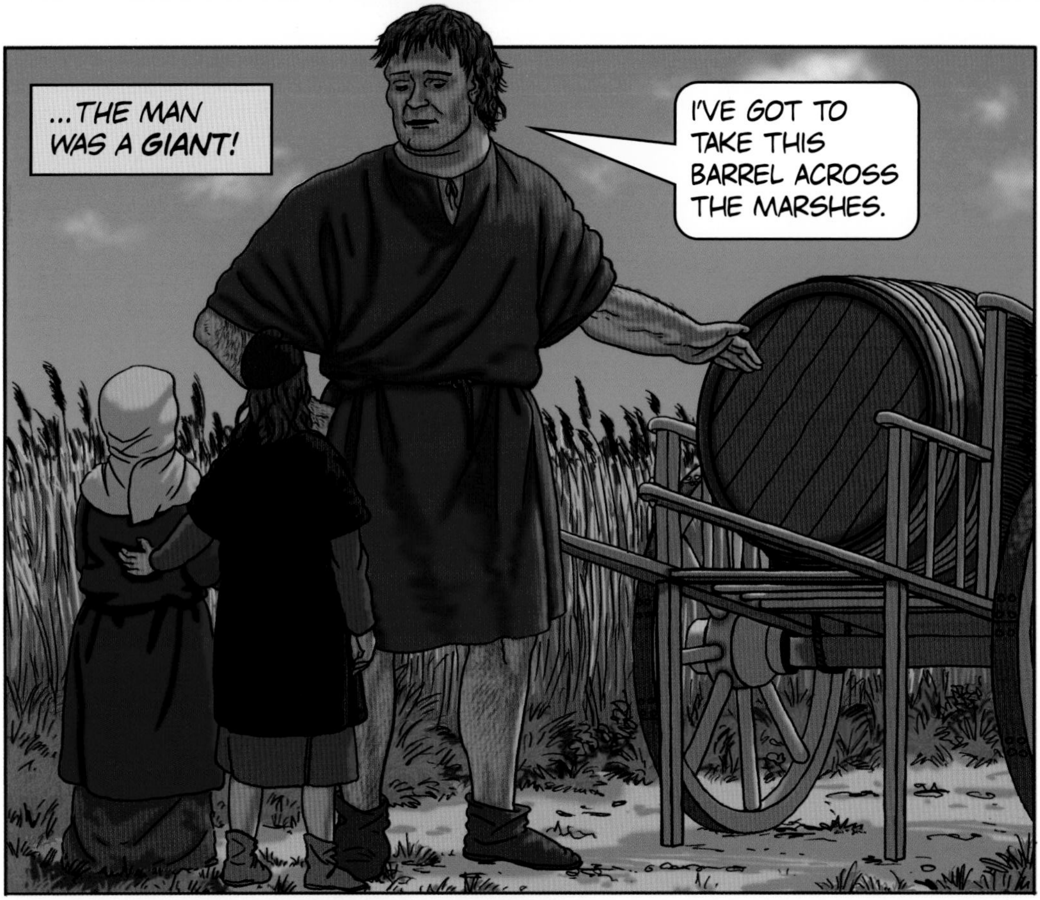
...THE MAN WAS A **GIANT!**
I'VE GOT TO TAKE THIS BARREL ACROSS THE MARSHES.

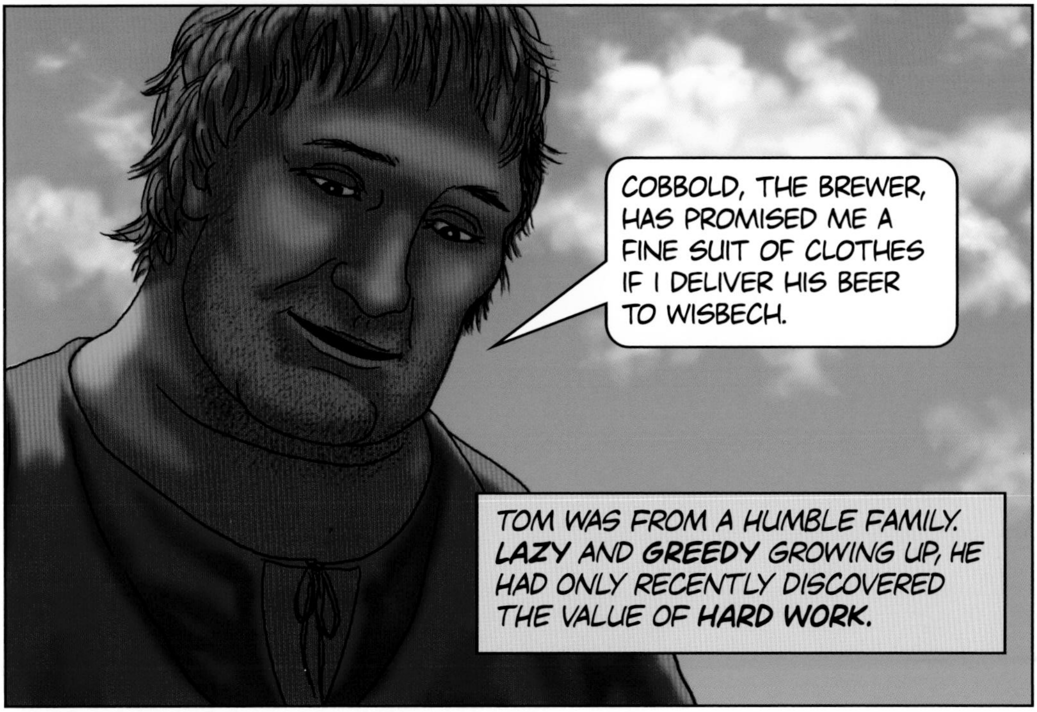
COBBOLD, THE BREWER, HAS PROMISED ME A FINE SUIT OF CLOTHES IF I DELIVER HIS BEER TO WISBECH.
TOM WAS FROM A HUMBLE FAMILY. **LAZY** AND **GREEDY** GROWING UP, HE HAD ONLY RECENTLY DISCOVERED THE VALUE OF **HARD WORK.**

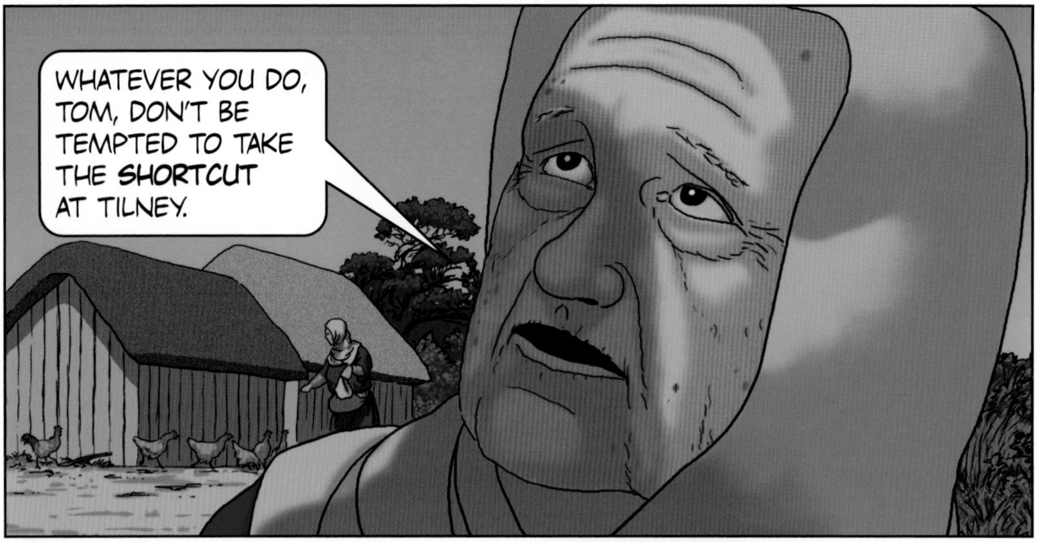
WHATEVER YOU DO, TOM, DON'T BE TEMPTED TO TAKE THE **SHORTCUT** AT TILNEY.

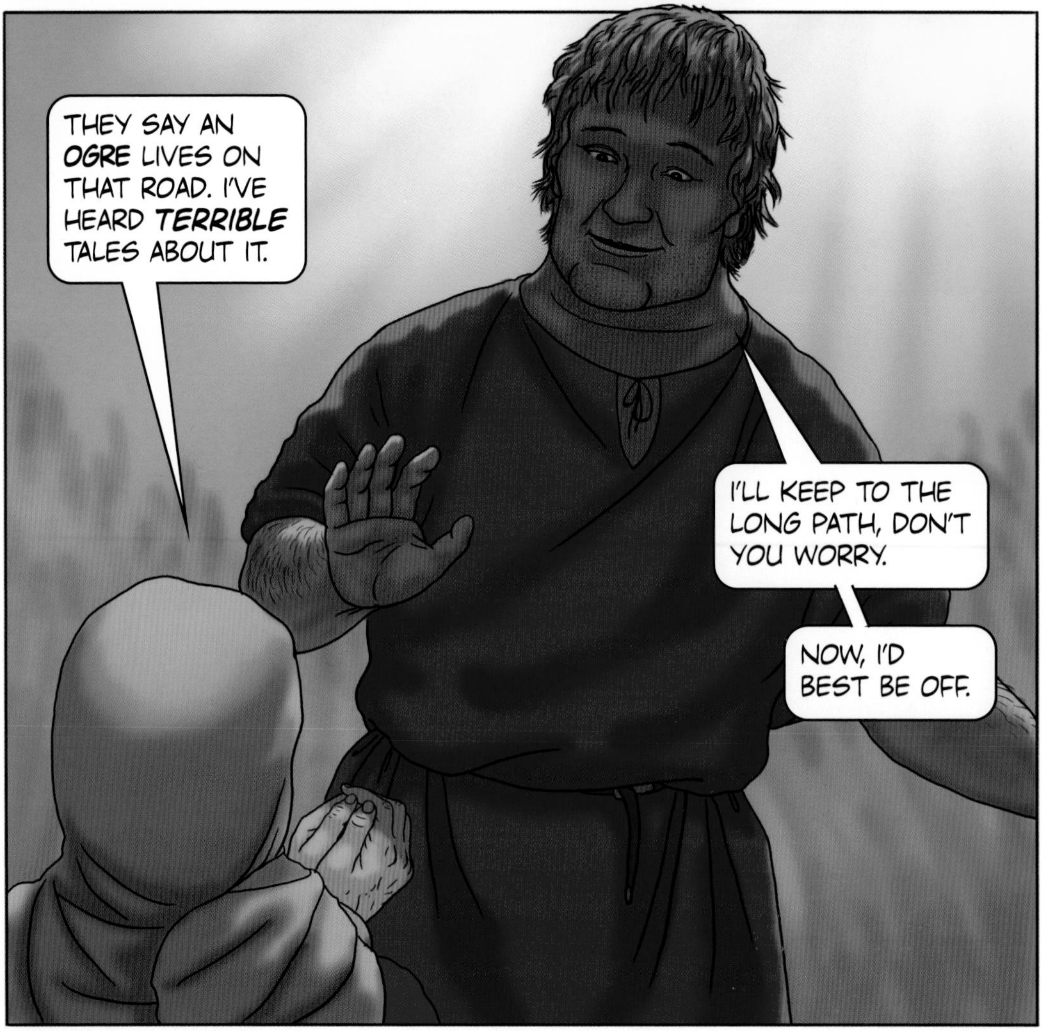
THEY SAY AN **OGRE** LIVES ON THAT ROAD. I'VE HEARD **TERRIBLE** TALES ABOUT IT.
I'LL KEEP TO THE LONG PATH, DON'T YOU WORRY.
NOW, I'D BEST BE OFF.

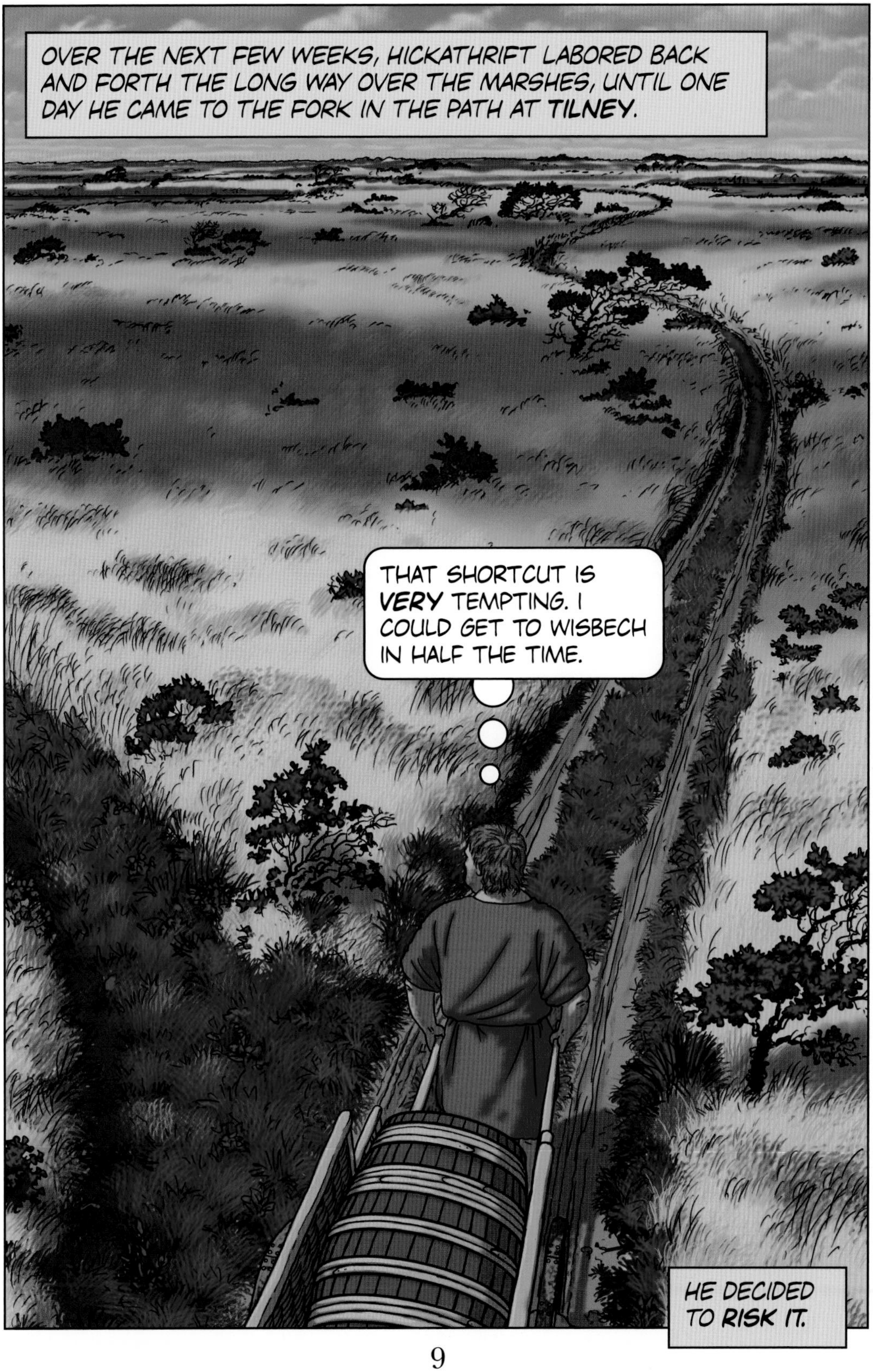
OVER THE NEXT FEW WEEKS, HICKATHRIFT LABORED BACK AND FORTH THE LONG WAY OVER THE MARSHES, UNTIL ONE DAY HE CAME TO THE FORK IN THE PATH AT **TILNEY**.
THAT SHORTCUT IS **VERY** TEMPTING. I COULD GET TO WISBECH IN HALF THE TIME.
HE DECIDED TO **RISK IT**.

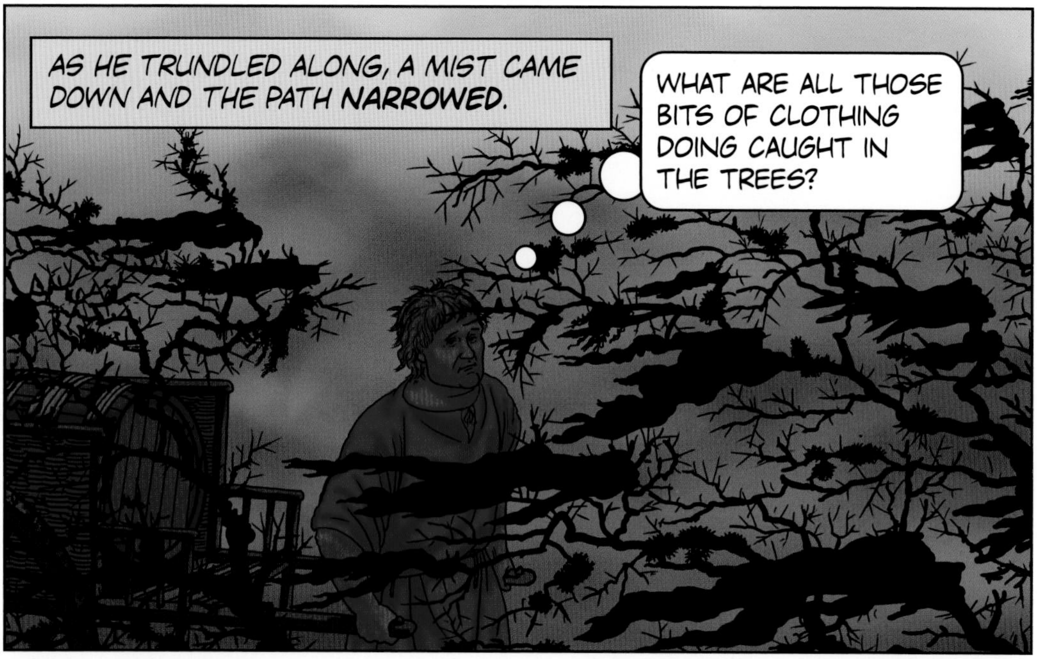
AS HE TRUNDLED ALONG, A MIST CAME DOWN AND THE PATH NARROWED.
WHAT ARE ALL THOSE BITS OF CLOTHING DOING CAUGHT IN THE TREES?

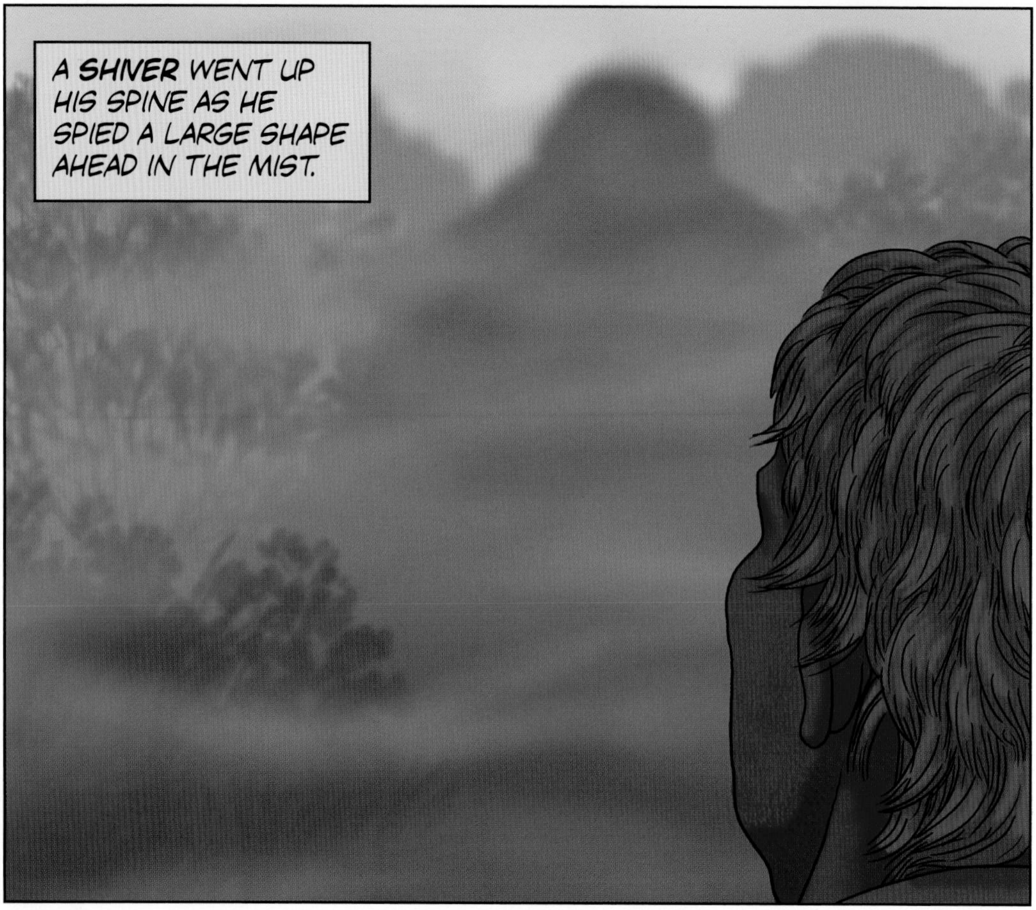
A SHIVER WENT UP HIS SPINE AS HE SPIED A LARGE SHAPE AHEAD IN THE MIST.

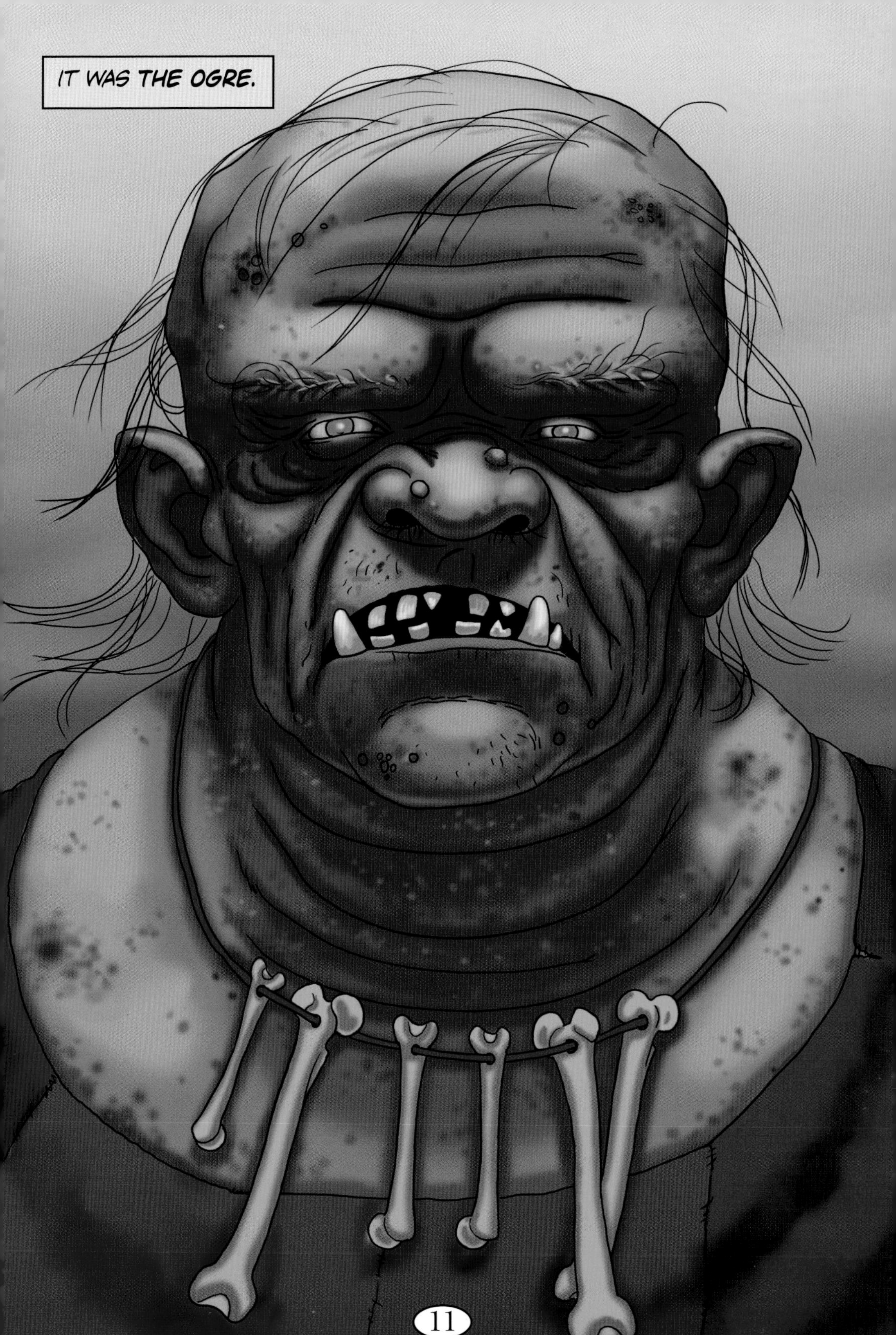
IT WAS THE OGRE.

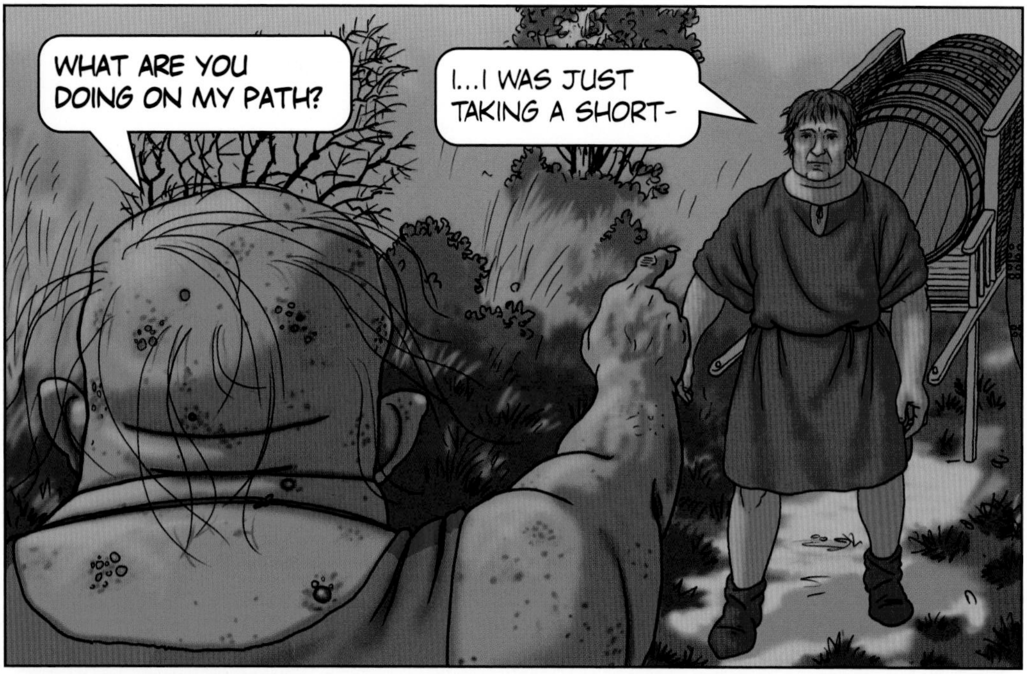
WHAT ARE YOU DOING ON MY PATH?
I...I WAS JUST TAKING A SHORT-

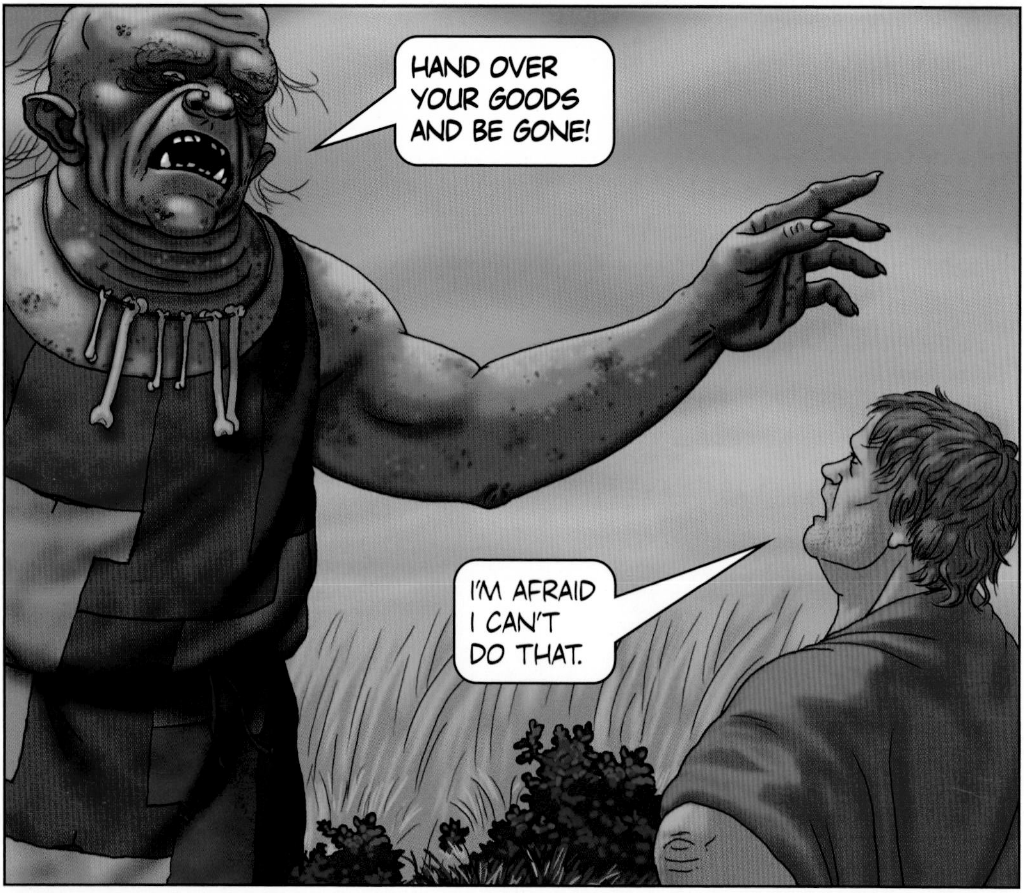
HAND OVER YOUR GOODS AND BE GONE!
I'M AFRAID I CAN'T DO THAT.

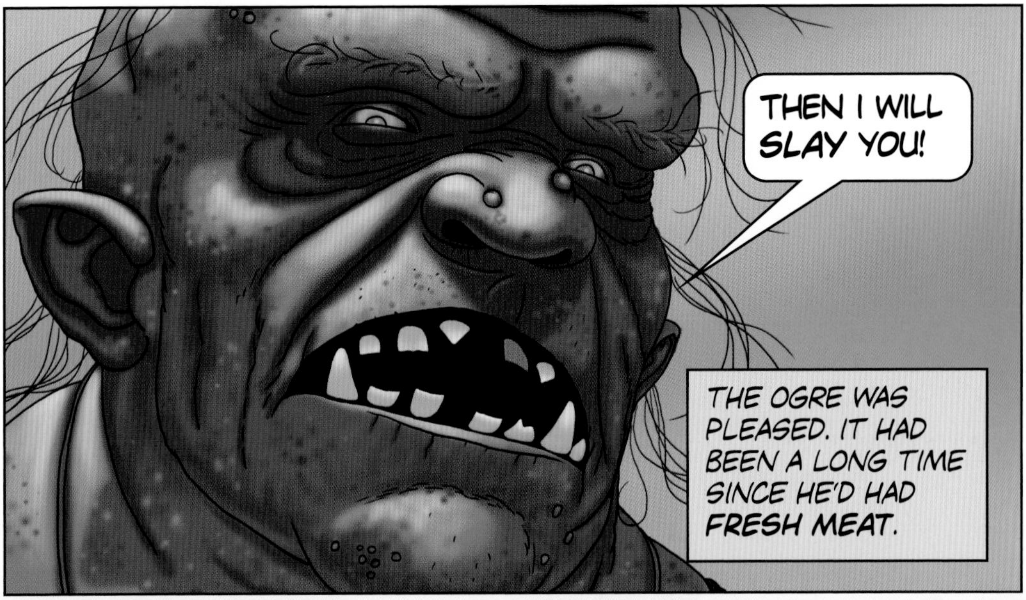
THEN I WILL SLAY YOU!
THE OGRE WAS PLEASED. IT HAD BEEN A LONG TIME SINCE HE'D HAD FRESH MEAT.

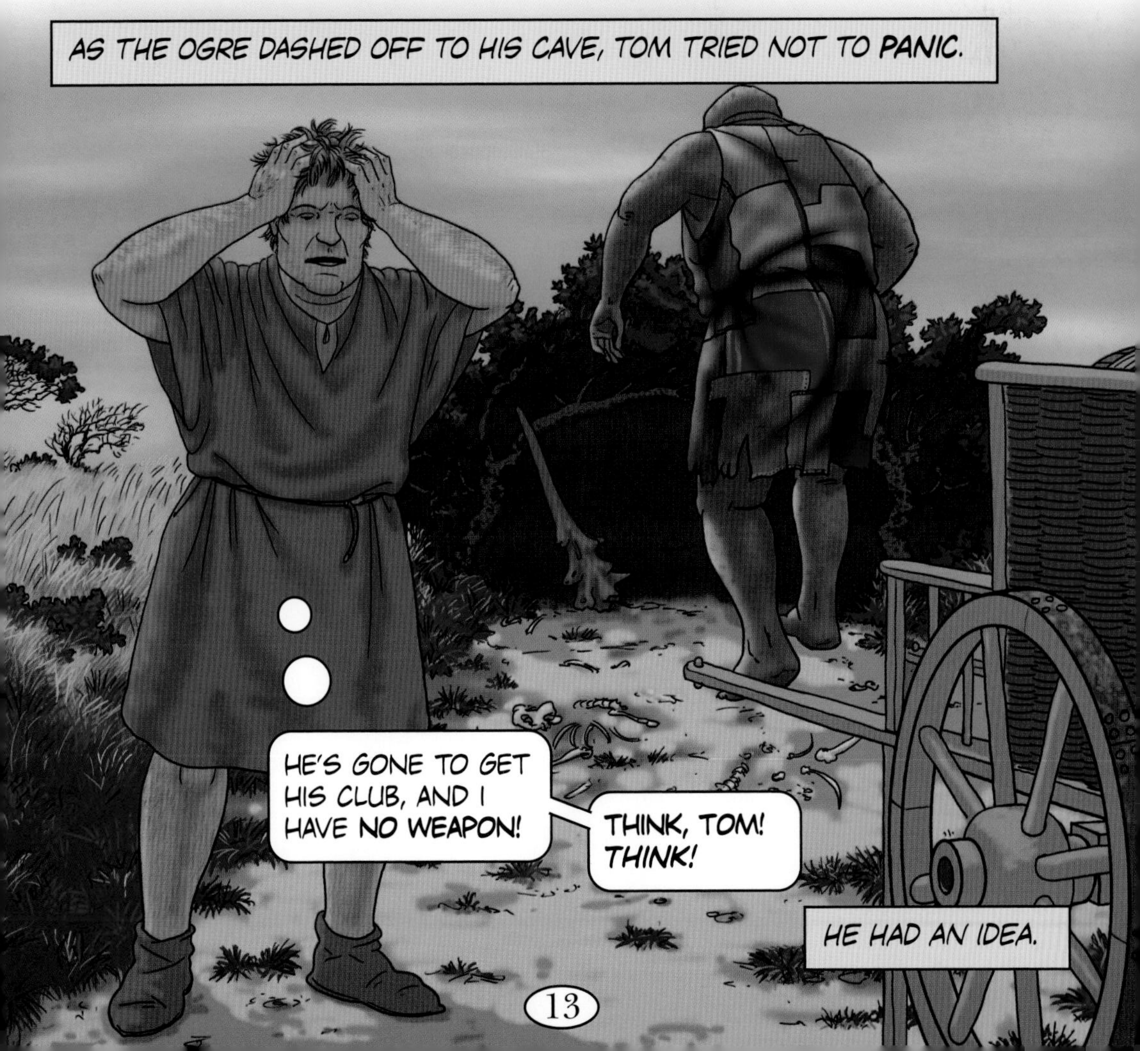
AS THE OGRE DASHED OFF TO HIS CAVE, TOM TRIED NOT TO PANIC.
HE'S GONE TO GET HIS CLUB, AND I HAVE NO WEAPON!
THINK, TOM! THINK!
HE HAD AN IDEA.

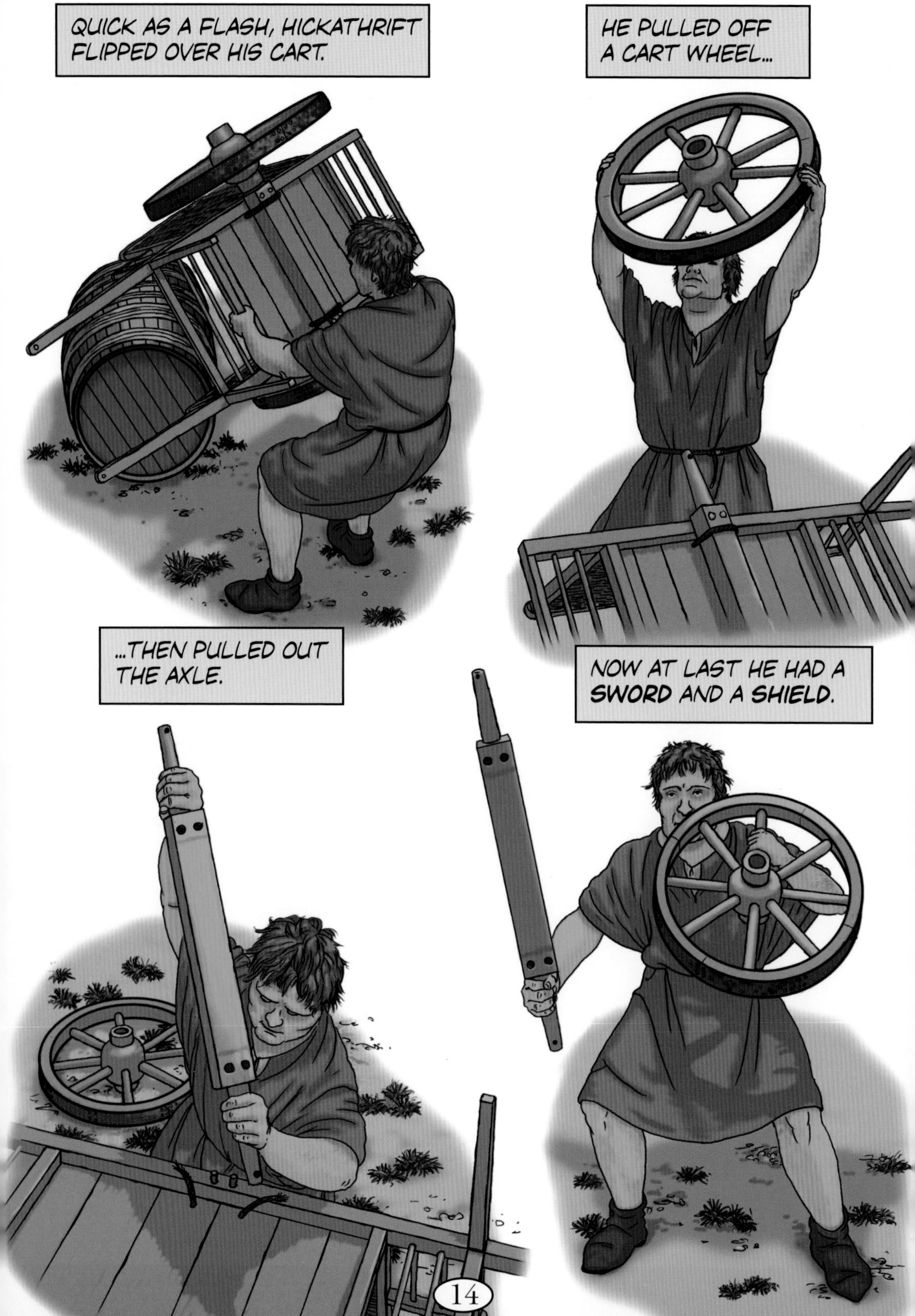
QUICK AS A FLASH, HICKATHRIFT FLIPPED OVER HIS CART.
HE PULLED OFF A CART WHEEL...
...THEN PULLED OUT THE AXLE.
NOW AT LAST HE HAD A **SWORD** AND A **SHIELD**.

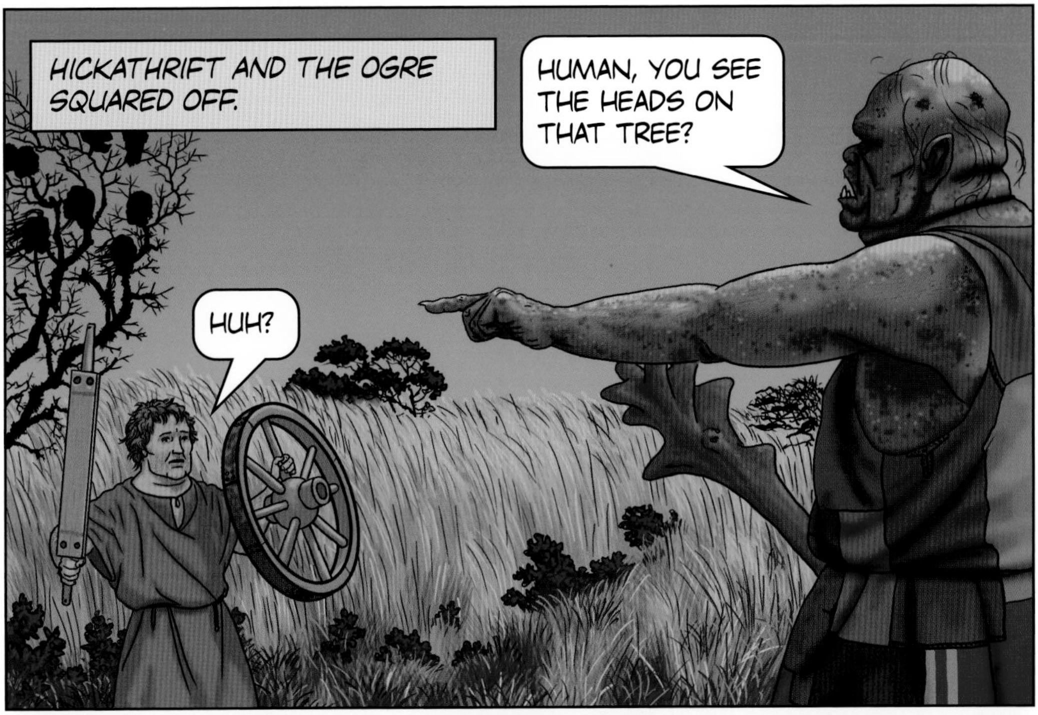
HICKATHRIFT AND THE OGRE SQUARED OFF.
HUMAN, YOU SEE THE HEADS ON THAT TREE?
HUH?

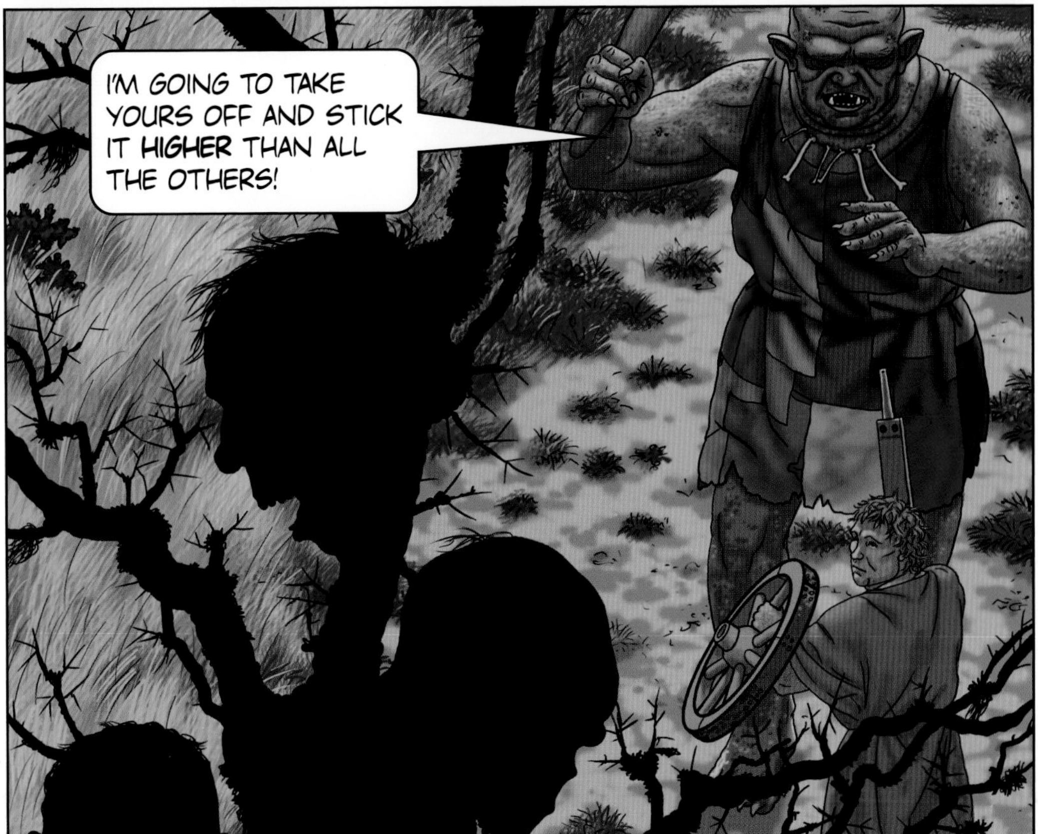
I'M GOING TO TAKE YOURS OFF AND STICK IT **HIGHER** THAN ALL THE OTHERS!

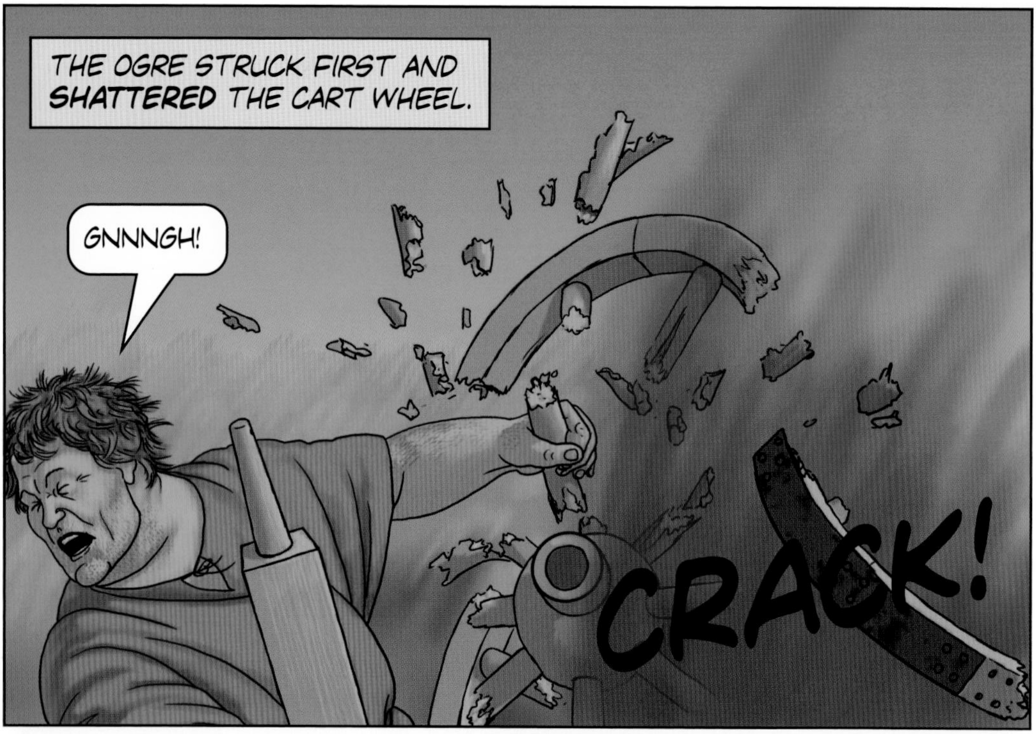
THE OGRE STRUCK FIRST AND SHATTERED THE CART WHEEL.
GNNNGH!
CRACK!

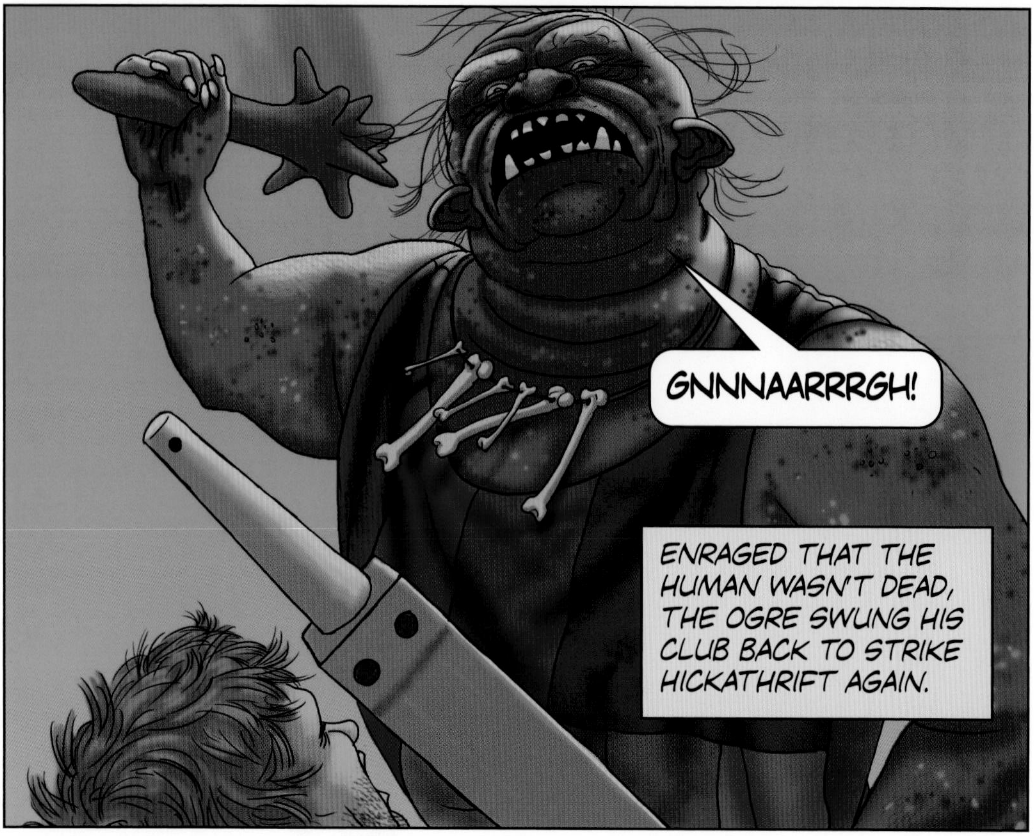
GNNNAARRRGH!
ENRAGED THAT THE HUMAN WASN'T DEAD, THE OGRE SWUNG HIS CLUB BACK TO STRIKE HICKATHRIFT AGAIN.

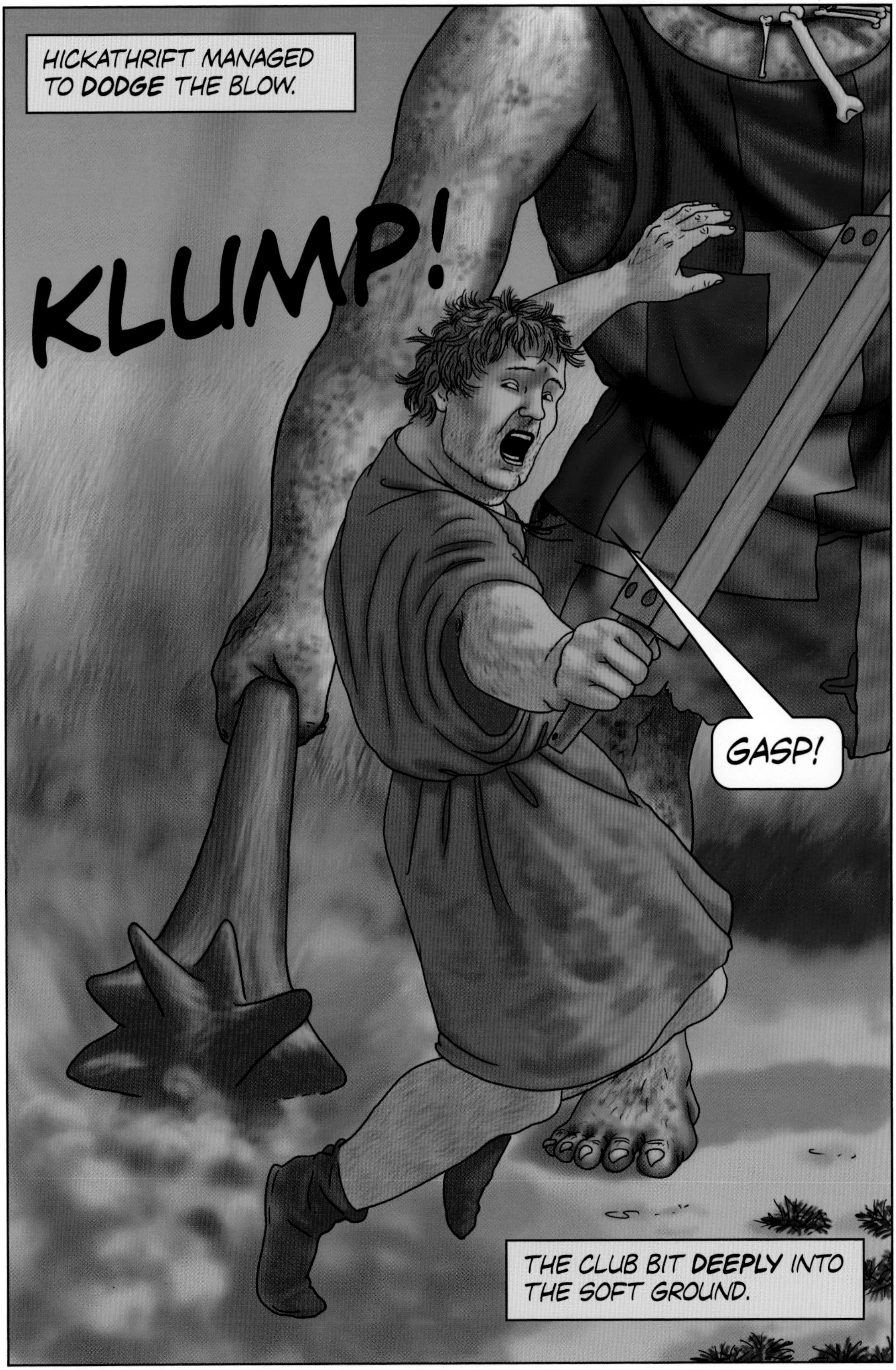
HICKATHRIFT MANAGED TO **DODGE** THE BLOW.
KLUMP!
GASP!
THE CLUB BIT **DEEPLY** INTO THE SOFT GROUND.

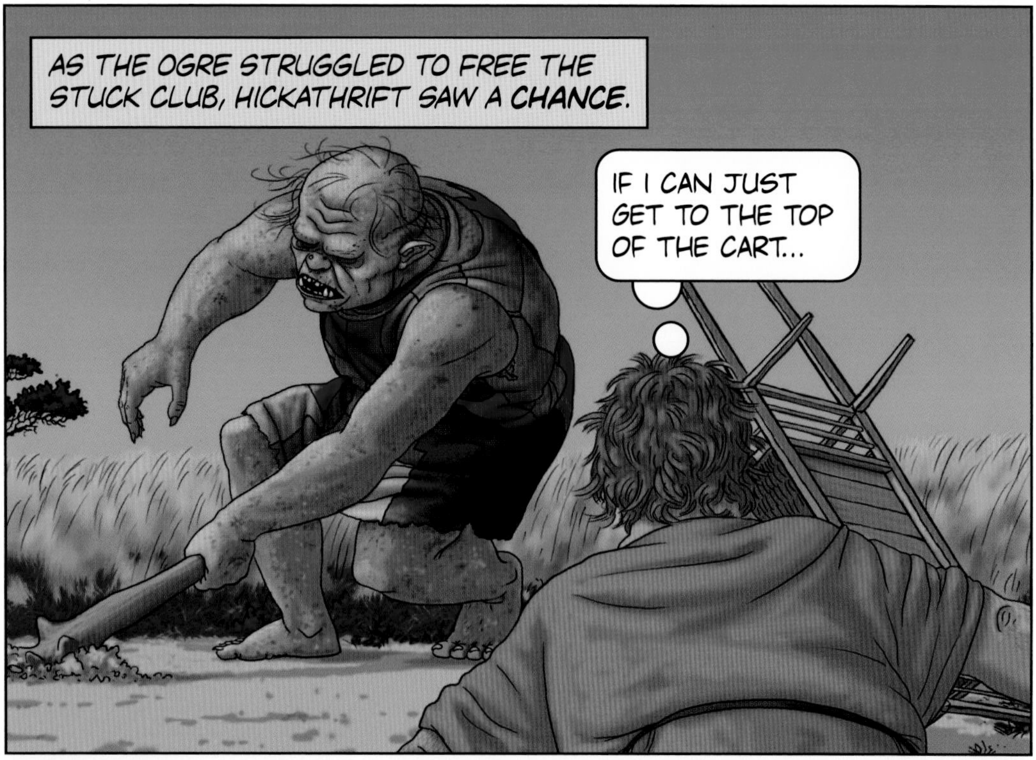
AS THE OGRE STRUGGLED TO FREE THE STUCK CLUB, HICKATHRIFT SAW A **CHANCE.**
IF I CAN JUST GET TO THE TOP OF THE CART...

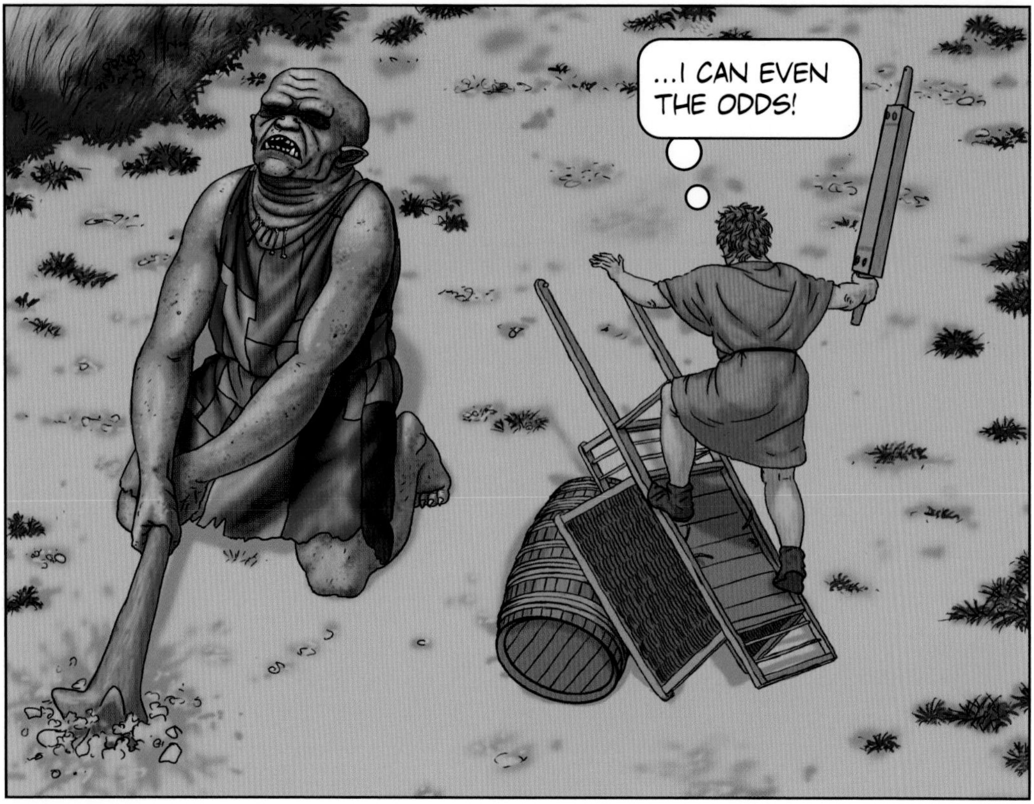
...I CAN EVEN THE ODDS!

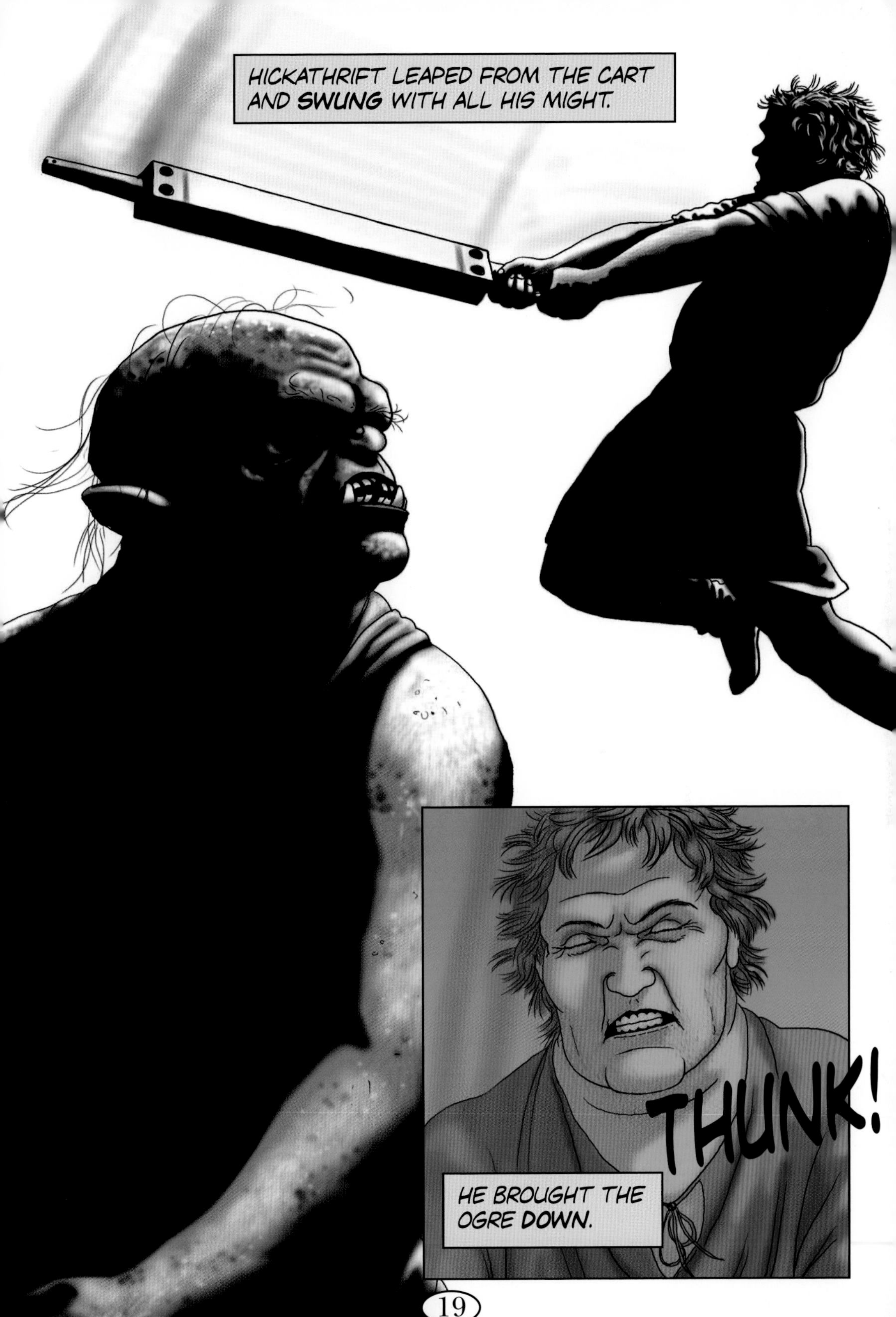
HICKATHRIFT LEAPED FROM THE CART AND SWUNG WITH ALL HIS MIGHT.
THUNK!
HE BROUGHT THE OGRE DOWN.

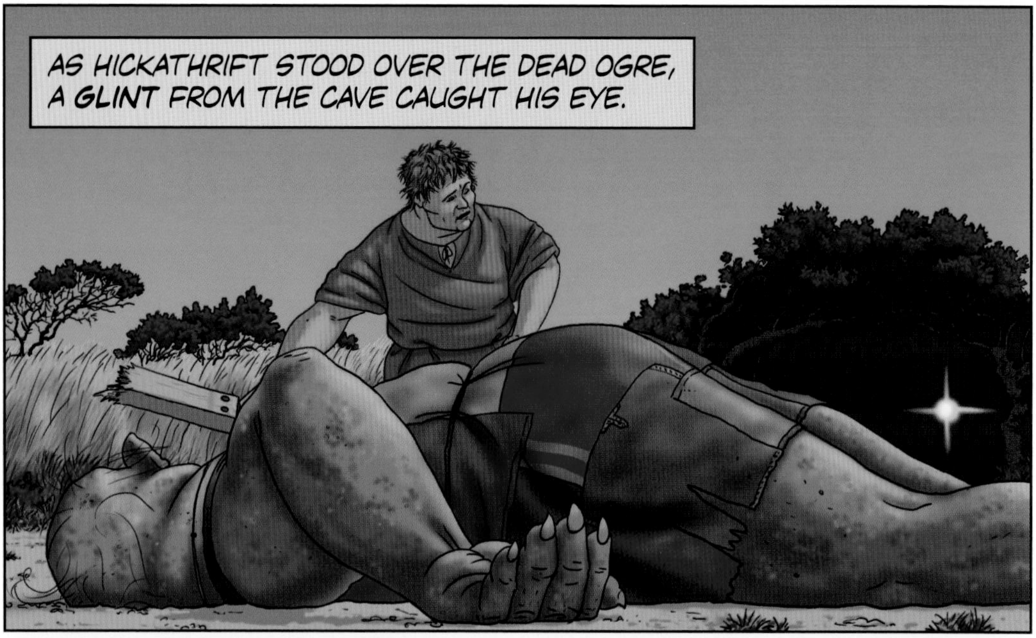
AS HICKATHRIFT STOOD OVER THE DEAD OGRE, A GLINT FROM THE CAVE CAUGHT HIS EYE.

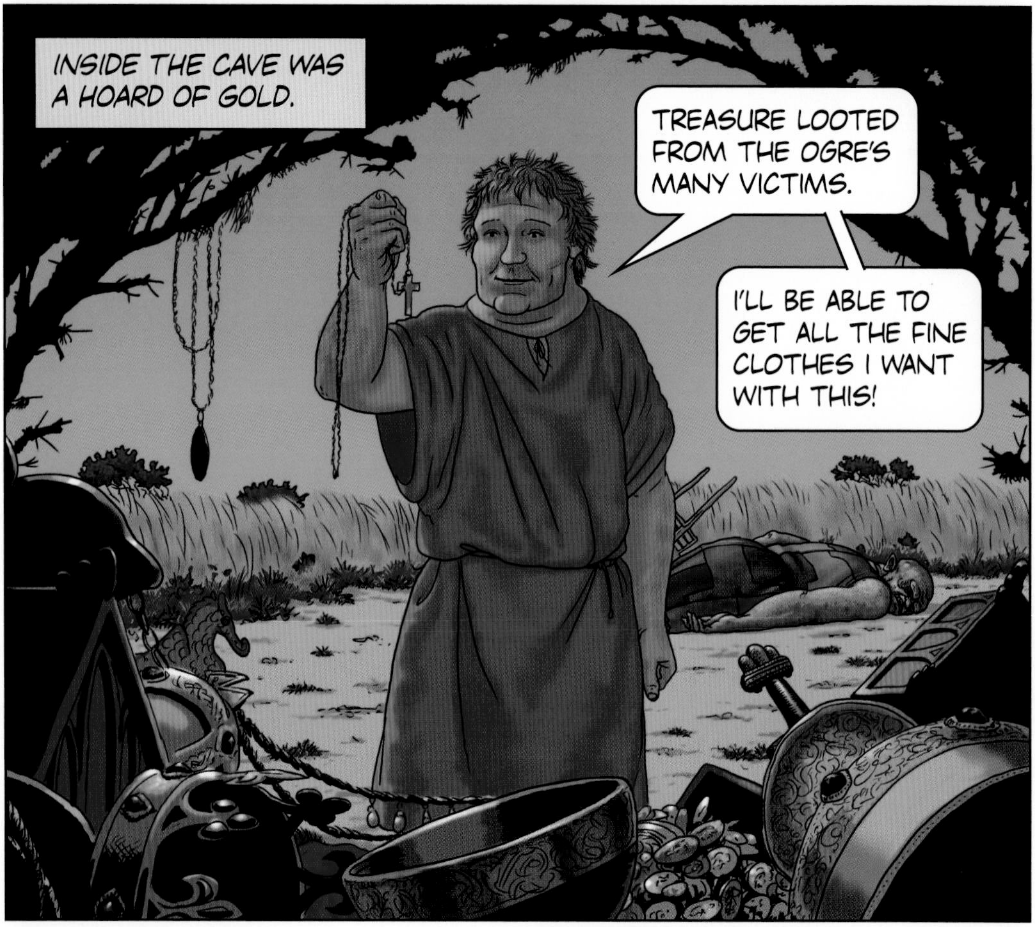
INSIDE THE CAVE WAS A HOARD OF GOLD.
TREASURE LOOTED FROM THE OGRE'S MANY VICTIMS.
I'LL BE ABLE TO GET ALL THE FINE CLOTHES I WANT WITH THIS!

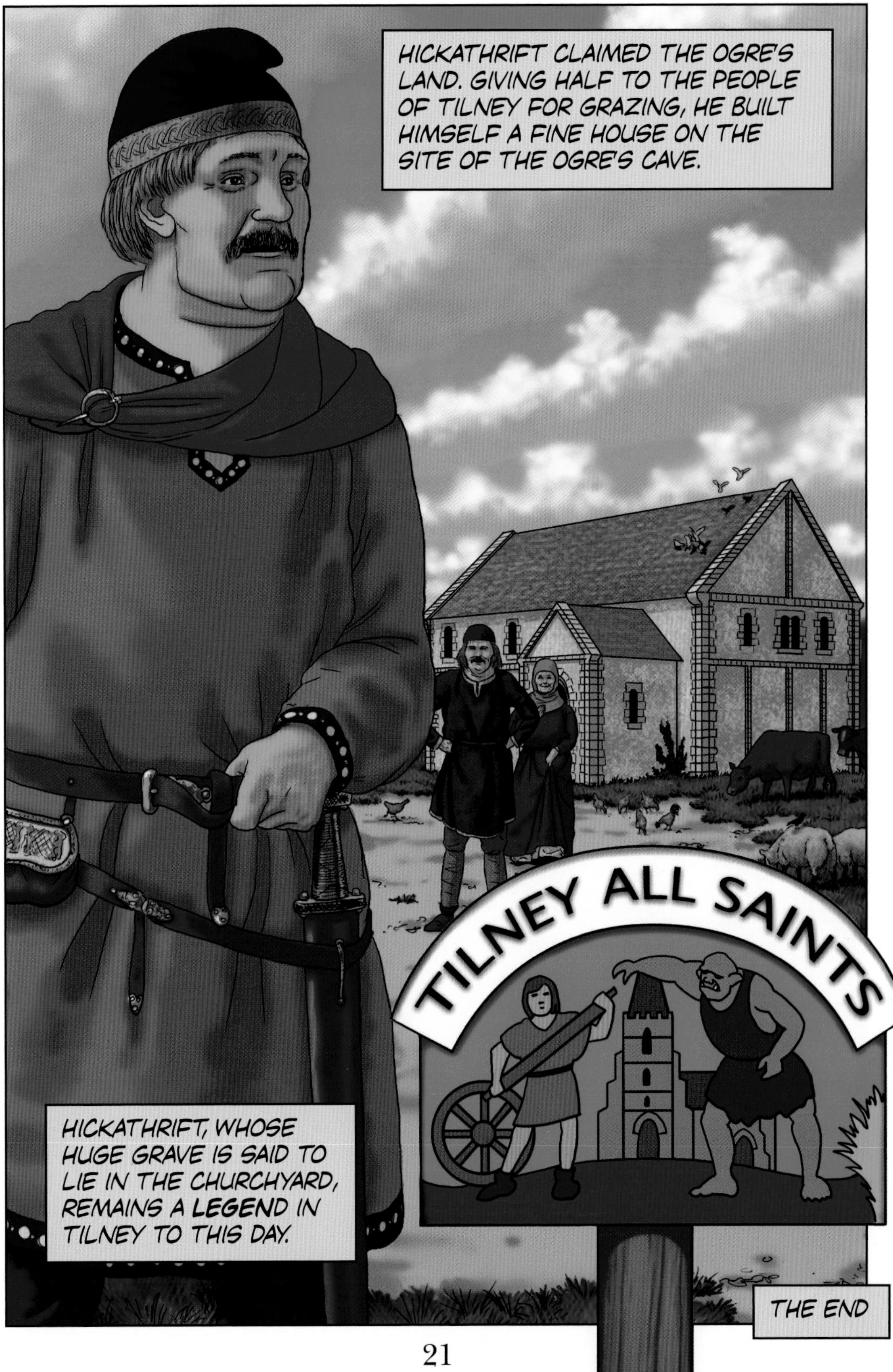
HICKATHRIFT CLAIMED THE OGRE'S LAND. GIVING HALF TO THE PEOPLE OF TILNEY FOR GRAZING, HE BUILT HIMSELF A FINE HOUSE ON THE SITE OF THE OGRE'S CAVE.
TILNEY ALL SAINTS
HICKATHRIFT, WHOSE HUGE GRAVE IS SAID TO LIE IN THE CHURCHYARD, REMAINS A **LEGEND** IN TILNEY TO THIS DAY.
THE END

Other Ogre Tales

Ogres are a fairly recent addition to the mythological bestiary. Although their stories are often bloodcurdlingly cruel, the heroes always win out in the end.

Hop-o'-My-Thumb

A fairy tale based on folklore. Seven brothers are abandoned in the forest by their poor parents. They are caught by a huge ogre, who plans to eat them. The smallest of the brothers, called Hop, defeats the ogre by stealing his magic boots.

The Ogre of Rashomon

An ogress (female ogre) haunts a gate at the Japanese city of Kyoto. A samurai cuts off the monster's arm. The ogress disguises herself as an old woman to get it back.

Momotoro and the Ogres

A Japanese folktale. Momotoro, the hero born from a peach, travels with friends to the island of ogres for a duel to the death.

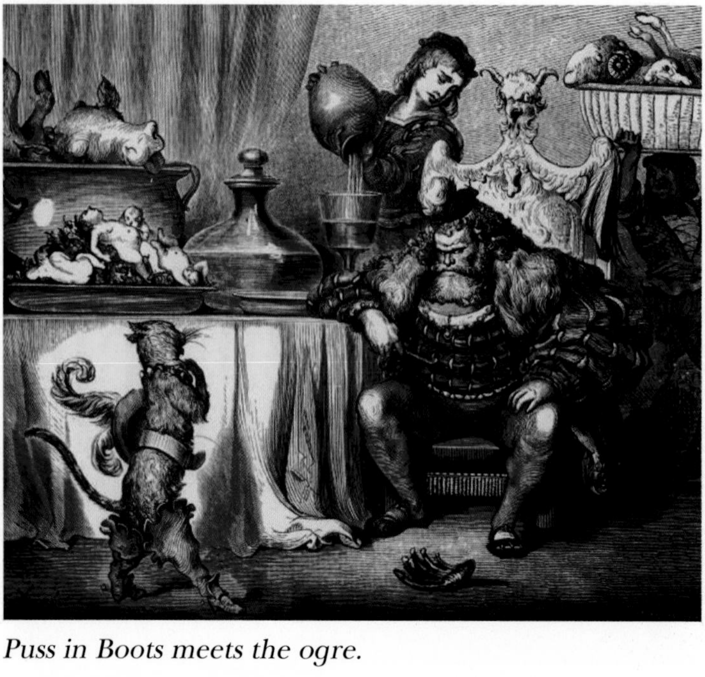

Puss in Boots meets the ogre.

Puss in Boots

First published in 1697. This is a famous tale of a clever cat who gains a castle for his master by tricking a shape-changing ogre. After the ogre changes into a lion, Puss tricks him into changing into a mouse and eats him!

GLOSSARY

axle A supporting bar or shaft on which a set of wheel revolves.

bestiary A collection of fables intended to teach a moral lesson, in which the characters are real or imaginary animals.

cunning Cleverness, skill, and ingenuity or even deception.

even the odds To make something more fair if two sides in a contest are uneven, for example in strength.

folklore Traditional beliefs, myths, and tales that are passed down through generations by word of mouth.

forerunner A person or thing that comes before another.

hoard A hidden supply of treasure or food, for example, stored for future use.

might Physical strength or power.

outwit To get the better of someone by cleverness or ingenuity.

prey To hunt, catch, or eat something for food.

slay To kill someone violently.

trundle To move along by, or as if by, rolling wheels.

Index